Contents

KUNG FU PANDA 2: ANNUAL 2012
A BANTAM BOOK 978 0 857 51051 8

First published in Great Britain by Bantam,
an imprint of Random House Children's Books
A Random House Group Company

This edition published 2011

1 3 5 7 9 10 8 6 4 2

Bantam Books are published by
Random House Children's Books,
61–63 Uxbridge Road, London W5 5SA

www.totallyrandombooks.co.uk
www.kidsatrandomhouse.co.uk

Addresses for companies within The Random House Group Limited can be found at:
www.randomhouse.co.uk/offices.htm

THE RANDOM HOUSE GROUP Limited Reg. No. 954009

A CIP catalogue record for this book is available from the British Library

Printed in Italy

MEET THE CHARACTERS

PO – Po is now the legendary Dragon Warrior. He loves noodles, kung fu, his friends and his dad more than ever. But when a dangerous band of wolves visit the Valley of Peace, Po has some strange memories that make him question where he came from – and who he really is.

MR PING – He couldn't be more proud of his panda son, and makes sure he has extra helpings of bean buns ready to feed the Dragon Warrior. Po's dad always has words of comfort when Po's feeling down.

MASTER SHIFU – Even though he has been elevated as the Valley's spiritual leader, Po's antics can still make Shifu chant, "Inner peace . . . Inner peace . . ." As he takes Po into the last and most important stage of his kung fu training, Shifu must teach Po to find inner peace himself.

THE FURIOUS FIVE

TIGRESS – She is the strongest and boldest of the kung fu Masters. She'd do anything to save the day. Underneath her iron-jawed exterior is a warm compassion that others seldom see.

MONKEY – Mischievous and playful, Monkey can surprise you with his cunning martial arts ability. This cheeky monkey likes a good joke, even in the heat of battle.

CRANE – Crane is a think first, punch second kind of bird, but his fellow kung fu Masters' safety is his priority. He's willing to risk his life to protect them.

VIPER – She's the softest and most feminine of the group. But don't let her gentle nature fool you. Viper can take down the most intimidating foe in the blink of an eye.

MANTIS – Mantis may be the smallest of the five, but nothing can strike fear into his brave little heart. He plays a key role in battling Lord Shen.

In Gongmen City ...

LORD SHEN – The albino peacock has created the most devastating weapon the world has ever known. It can defeat everything, even kung fu. Shen also hopes that it will destroy the prophecy that "a warrior of black and white" would one day defeat him ...

SOOTHSAYER – The old goat was a loyal and faithful servant to Lord Shen's parents. Blessed with the ability to foresee the future, her prediction of Shen's fate has made her pretty unpopular.

BOSS WOLF – Boss Wolf built an army of wolves loyal to Shen. Utterly cruel and ruthless, just like his master, he is Shen's most loyal servant, military strategist and trusted right hand.

MASTER THUNDERING RHINO – He protects the vast metropolis of Gongmen City. As head of the Kung Fu Council, he is revered for his wisdom, kind humour and good deeds.

MASTER STORMING OX – This trusted member of the Kung Fu Council is famous for his bravery. Once, in sinking rice fields, he battled 72 bandits with his bare horns.

MASTER CROC – He is known for his many victories, such as the time his blades silenced the badger bandits who dishonoured his mother. Like Master Ox, he is one of Po's most-loved heroes.

ALL PATHS LEAD TO FOOD... OR DO THEY?

Po is hungry . . . as always . . . but can you help him discover the path to noodle glory?

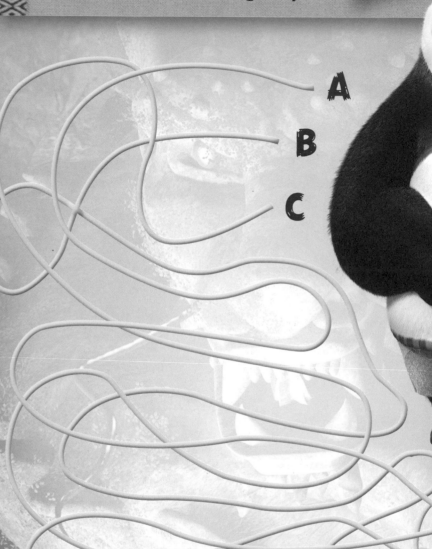

A

B

C

ANSWER: ___

ANSWERS ON PAGE 61!

10

REBUILD THE DREAM TEAM!

Using the silhouette as a guide, can you work out which order Po, Shifu and the Furious Five should stand in, to create a totem pole of kung fu power?

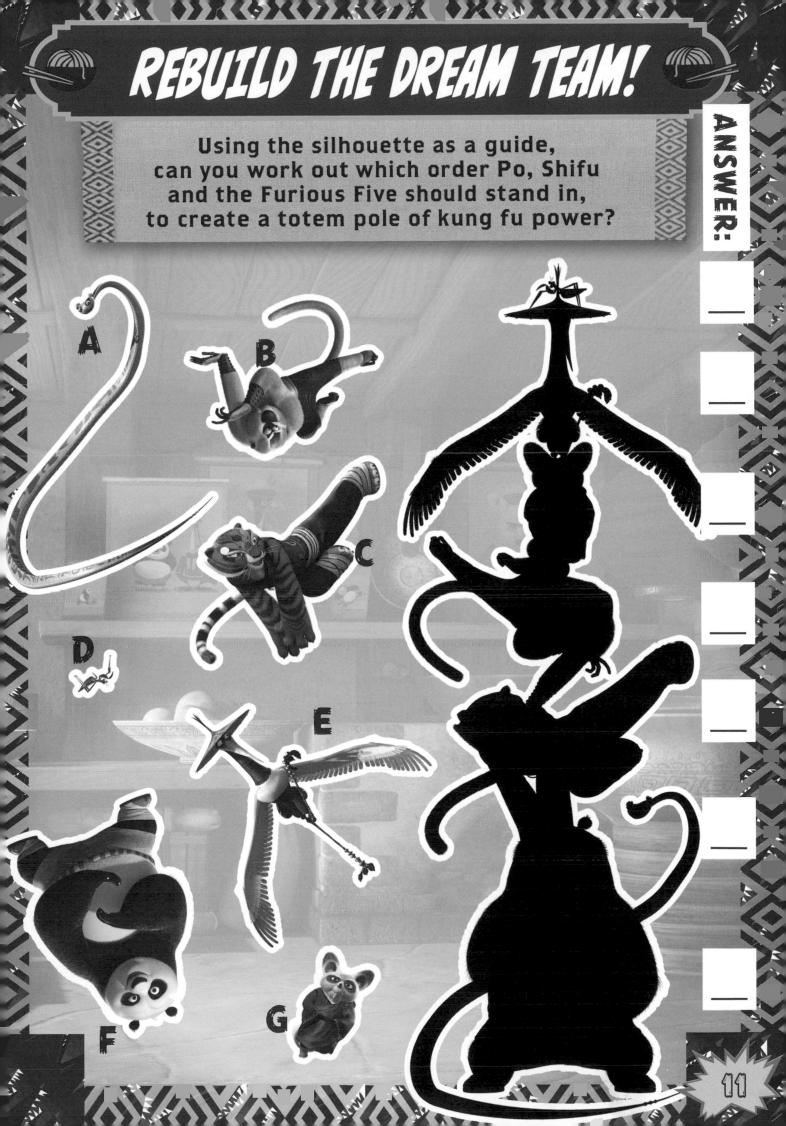

11

A LONG TIME AGO AND FAR, FAR AWAY . . .

Long ago, the Peacocks of Gongmen City created a thing of great beauty: fireworks. For generations the rockets brought joy, but the Peacocks' ambitious young heir, Shen, saw a potential for fear and destruction.

Worried, Shen's parents turned to Soothsayer. When the wise goat foresaw Shen being stopped by "a mighty warrior of black and white", Shen embarked on a terrible rampage, ridding China of all its pandas. Ashamed of their only son, Shen's parents banished him. But Shen swore he'd return, wreak havoc and rule Gongmen City . . .

PRESENT DAY
Years passed by. Shen gathered an army of ruthless wolves to seek out metal and black powder to create the ultimate weapon. But the peacock had forgotten what Soothsayer forewarned . . .

Far away, it was a beautiful day in the Valley of Peace. But loud cries bellowed from the barracks.
"Ahh! It's too horrible," Viper grimaced.

The Furious Five stared at Po with a mix of shock, horror and pride as the panda gave them a satisfied smile . . . bulging with 40 bean buns!

Still munching, Po headed to the Dragon Grotto to find Master Shifu balancing on the tip of his staff. "Inner peace. Inner peace," Shifu chanted as Po rushed in and splashed water everywhere, wrecking the calm. Po then watched in amazement as a water droplet fell from the ceiling, and at the very last minute, his kung fu master reached up, caught the drip and redirected it onto a nearby plant.

"AWESOME!" cried Po in astonishment. "How did you do that?"

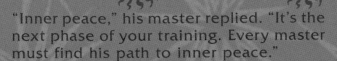

"Inner peace," his master replied. "It's the next phase of your training. Every master must find his path to inner peace."

"I'm pretty peaceful in my innards," Po smiled, patting his tummy, "Inner peace you're going down! Alright! It's on!"

Suddenly, the gong sounded from the valley and Tigress came rushing in.

"Bandits! Approaching the musician's village!" she cried.

The village was in chaos. One bunny madly rang the bell to sound the alarm.

"Get all the metal you can find!" Boss Wolf yelled at his troops.

Villagers fled in terror as the wolves stole metallic instruments, chimes and gongs. As the last pieces of metal were gathered up, an awesome sound rang throughout the village. "WAA HOOOOO!!!!" screamed Po, as the Furious Five exploded into action!

Although shocked to see a panda, Boss Wolf quickly sent his troops into battle. Mantis saved a blind bunny from a wolf's swinging sword . . . Viper elegantly sent a mace-wielding bandit bouncing off a drum . . . while Po and Tigress kicked some serious wolf butt!

Panicked, Boss Wolf howled a signal to a gorilla hidden by the mists above the village. With grappling hooks, he pulled their metal loot high into the air.

Boss Wolf, battle hammer raised, readied himself to attack.

"I got this," Po said, focused.

As Boss Wolf swung, Po saw an eye symbol on the wolf's uniform. Suddenly, his head started spinning and all he could see was a bright red flash. He saw a red eye . . . Heard a baby cry . . . And saw a mother panda holding a radish . . .

"Po!" yelled Tigress, but the wolf's battle hammer sent Po flying, knocking Tigress and several bunnies flat.

"Sweet dreams, panda!" laughed Boss Wolf as he left the village.

"What happened?" asked Tigress.

"I don't know," Po replied, completely confused.

ONE GOOSE'S RUBBISH IS ANOTHER GOOSE'S TREASURE

Po knew that the only person who could help solve his strange flashback was his dad. So he set off to the Dragon Warrior Noodles and Tofu Shop to talk to Mr Ping.

The shop was bustling, full of happy customers keen to eat the valley's best noodles in the very restaurant where the mighty Dragon Warrior once worked.

"Feet of Fury!" beamed one bunny.

"The Dragon Warrior's Mop! He mopped these very floors!" cried another, as both bunnies reached out to touch it.

"Ahh! Ahh! No touching! You'll get the mop dirty!" cried Mr Ping. Suddenly all the customers became silent as they turned to face the door.

"The Dragon Warrior is here!" they all whispered and gasped.

Mr Ping rushed up to his son and gave him a huge hug.

"You should have told me you were coming," he cried. "I would have saved you some stinky tofu!"

In the kitchen, Mr Ping started to prepare some dinner but Po wasn't hungry.

"Uh, I had this crazy vision . . . I think I saw my mum. And me . . . as a baby?" Po mumbled. He struggled to get the next question out. "Dad, where did I come from?"
Mr Ping thought long and hard. "I think it's time I told you something I should have told you a long time ago," he said carefully. "You might have been, kind of, a–, a–, adopted."

"I knew it!" cried Po.

"You knew?" replied Mr Ping. "Who told you?"

"No-one," Po answered. "I mean, come on Dad."

Mr Ping gently pulled a radish basket out from under the counter. "You came from this," he said quietly. Mr Ping explained that many years ago, he had gone out to collect his weekly vegetable delivery to find an empty box of radishes that contained a very hungry baby panda.

"There was no note," Mr Ping explained. "But of course you could have eaten it, along with all the radishes."

No one claimed the baby panda, so Mr Ping fed him, washed him, fed him again and then tried – in vain – to put pants on him.

"And then I made a decision that would change my life forever," announced Mr Ping. "To make my soup without radishes! And to raise you as my own son Xiao Po, my little panda."

And Mr Ping admitted that from that moment on, his soup – and his life – had been much sweeter.

But Po still had many questions. "Like, how did I ever fit in this tiny basket? Why didn't I like pants? Who am I?"

AN ENEMY AT THE GATES

Far away in Gongmen City's Palace courtyard, Master Croc and Master Storming Ox were sparring in front of Master Thundering Rhino. Their kung fu moves were as impressive as the legends surrounding their mighty deeds.

From outside, a cloaked figure entered the gates.

Soothsayer watched from the side of the courtyard. Shen caught her eye, determined to prove how wrong her prophecy was.

"What do you want, Shen?" asked Master Rhino.

"What is rightfully mine. Gongmen City," the bird retorted.

"Shen?" Masters Croc and Ox gasped.

"Good afternoon gentlemen," said the peacock. "Now we've got the pleasantries out of the way, please leave my house."

"Your house?" Master Ox replied in surprise.

"Yes. Didn't you see the peacock on the front door?" Shen sneered.

"Gongmen is under the stewardship of the Masters Council and we will protect it. Even from you." Master Rhino said firmly.

"I'm so glad you feel that way," laughed Shen. "Otherwise I would have dragged that here for nothing."

An army of wolves poured through the Palace gates dragging a huge wooden crate.

"It's a gift!" yelled Shen. "It's your parting gift, in that it will part you. Part of you here, part of you there."

"You insolent fool!" cried Master Ox as he and Master Croc leapt at Shen. But the bird was too quick – feather-shaped metal blades flew out of his cloak's sleeves! More of Shen's blades were flung at Rhino, but the kung fu master sent the bird flying.

"You are no match for my kung fu," cried Master Rhino.

"I agree," sneered Shen, "but this is." Shen opened the crate, revealing a black metal tube with a dragon's head.
He scraped his claw along the barrel and the sparks ignited the fuse. All Master Rhino could do was to watch helplessly as . . . KABOOM!

Back in the Jade Palace, Master Shifu shared the bad news with Po and the Five that Master Rhino had been killed. Tigress couldn't believe her ears. "Rhino's Iron Horn Defence is impervious to any technique."

Shifu explained. "It was no technique. Lord Shen has created a weapon, one that breathes fire and spits metal. Unless he is stopped this could mean the end of kung fu."

"But I just got kung fu!" exclaimed Po.

"And now you must save it," replied Shifu. "Remember Dragon Warrior. If you are at peace you can do anything."

Down in the valley, Mr Ping gave Po a huge travel pack, crammed with vegetables, cookies, buns and his Furious Five action figures.

"Don't worry Mr Ping," reassured Tigress. "He will be back before you can say 'noodles.'"

Mr Ping watched sadly as Po and the Five left the valley to try and stop Shen.

2011: YEAR OF THE RABBIT!

What Chinese Year were you and your friends and family born? Do you share characteristics with that Chinese Year's animal? Find out below!

RAT

Born in: 1924, 1936, 1948, 1960, 1972, 1984, 1996 or 2008

You are a very honest person with great ambitions. You love reading and writing – did you know some of the world's greatest writers were born in the Year of the Rat?

OX

Born in: 1925, 1937, 1949, 1961, 1973, 1985, 1997 or 2009

You're a very inspiring person who is a natural leader – you could become a kung fu Master! You have great patience and show signs of mastering "inner peace."

TIGER

Born in: 1926, 1938, 1950, 1962, 1974, 1986, 1998 or 2010

Just like Tigress, you are courageous, curious but also sensitive. You're very much a live wire who loves to throw yourself into everyday life.

RABBIT

Born in: 1927, 1939, 1951, 1963, 1975, 1987, 1999 or 2011

You're a lucky soul, very observant, and adults will be happy to hear that if you're born in the year of the rabbit, you're helpful at home.

DRAGON

Born in: 1928, 1940, 1952, 1964, 1976, 1988, 2000 or 2012

With a huge passion for life, year of the Dragon people are fearless. Outspoken, you're destined to lead others and to make your dreams come true.

SNAKE

Born in: 1929, 1941, 1953, 1965, 1977, 1989, 2001 or 2013

You are the thinker of the Chinese cycle, a great philosopher. Intelligent, elegant and a great planner. Like Viper, you have a tender heart but aren't afraid to fight for what's right.

HORSE

Born in: 1930, 1942, 1954, 1966, 1978, 1990, 2002 or 2014

Highly spirited, you love having adventures. Any challenges that you face in life, you're more than capable of solving them yourself.

SHEEP

Born in: 1931, 1943, 1955, 1967, 1979, 1991, 2003 or 2015

You bring out the creativeness in everyone around you. A sensitive and imaginative artist, you have a romantic view of the world.

MONKEY

Born in: 1932, 1944, 1956, 1968, 1980, 1992, 2004 or 2016

Enthusiastic at all times, you really are bright-eyed and bushy-tailed. Naturally, monkeys are mischievous, but their joking around is loved by all.

ROOSTER

Born in: 1933, 1945, 1957, 1969, 1981, 1993, 2005 or 2017

You love to learn: finding out about the world around you is your most favourite thing. Neat and tidy, you find self-discipline very easy compared to others.

DOG

Born in: 1934, 1946, 1958, 1970, 1982, 1994, 2006 or 2018

Loyal, playful and generous with your friends and family, you are a pillar of strength for them all. Helping others makes you very happy, just like a heroic hound!

PIG

Born in: 1935, 1947, 1959, 1971, 1983, 1995, 2007 or 2019

You are a noble, polite soul who enjoys making friends. You also help others make great connections with like-minded people.

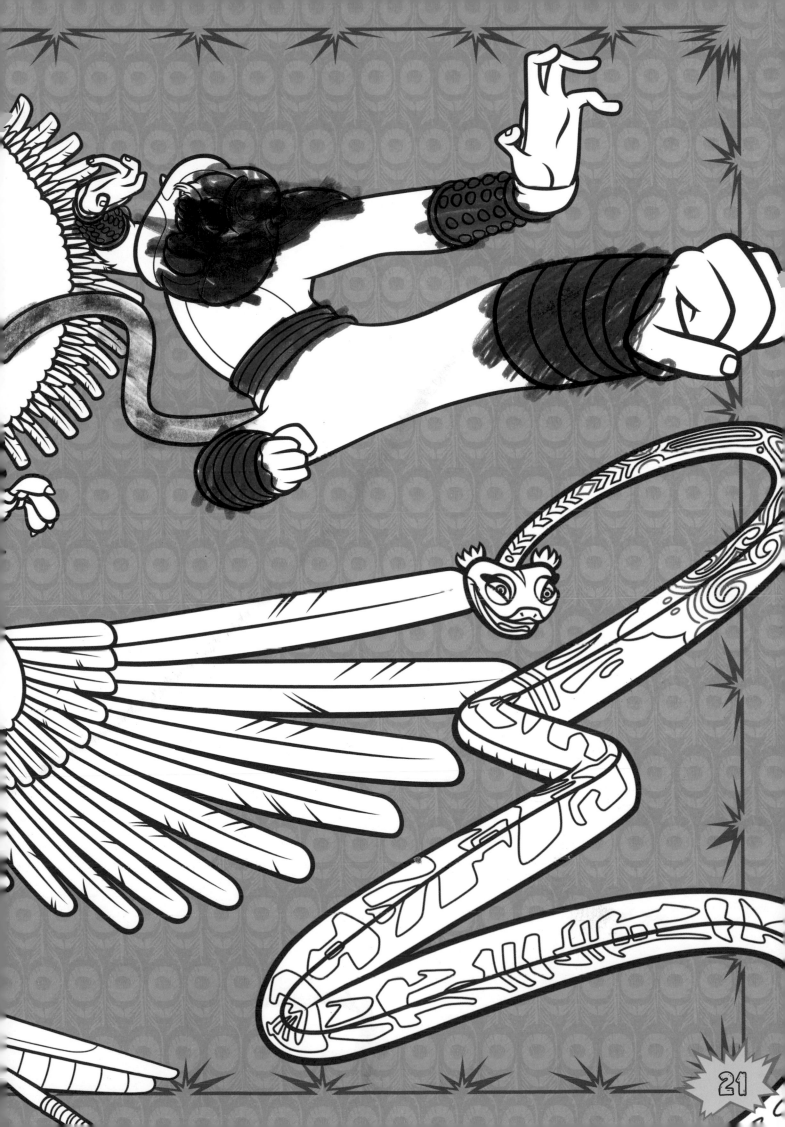

ON THE ROAD TO GONGMEN CITY

Po and the Furious Five made the treacherous journey to Gongmen City.

They crossed rocky plains . . . Trekked down sheer peaks . . . They climbed up sheer mountain rock faces . . . Some of the Five found it easier than others.

Deserts of scorching sand under a blazing hot sun challenged the team . . . Until they found the river that would carry them to Shen!

Meanwhile in Gongmen City, Lord Shen watched from the top of the Palace tower, while wolf soldiers wheeled barrels of black powder towards the fireworks factory.

Nearby, exhausted from their journey, the Five slept peacefully as they sailed down the Yangtze River towards Gongmen City. But the Dragon Warrior was having a nightmare . . .

In the dream, he spotted two pandas.

"Mum? Dad? Is that you?" he called out. But in his dream, Po's mum and dad weren't pleased to see him.

"We replaced you dear. With this lovely radish," Po's dream-mum told him.

"It's quiet, polite, and frankly, does better kung fu," said Po's dream-dad as the radish knocked poor Po to the ground with impressive kung fu.

"Aaahhh . . ." cried Po as he woke up with a start. He sighed and crawled out of the cabin.

"Radish, radish, radish . . ." he grumbled as he punched the mast. Drops of water fell from the sail and dripped onto his head.

"Inner peace," he chanted, while he mimicked Shifu's tai chi motions. But Po couldn't master the water droplet technique.

"Arrggghhhhhhhh!!!" cried Po in frustration.

"Ahem . . ." interrupted Tigress. "The mast is not a worthy opponent," she said as she solemnly held out her paws and faced Po.

"Um, OK," mumbled Po. He punched Tigress's palm hard but her arm didn't budge. Po held his sore fist in his other hand.

"I think I prefer the mast," he grumbled.

Tigress explained that as a young tiger she had trained by punching the ironwood trees around the Jade Palace, and now she felt nothing. "Again," Tigress instructed.

"Hyah," Po cried as he unleashed another punch.

"Po, why are you really out here?" Tigress asked, gently.

"I just found out my dad isn't my real dad," Po confessed.

"Your dad. The goose," Tigress paused. "That must have come as quite a shock."

"So what are you guys talking about?" asked Mantis, as the rest of the Five appeared on the deck.

"Po's having daddy issues," replied Viper.

"Man, I'm so lucky," said Mantis. "I don't have any problems with my dad. Maybe it's because Mom ate his head before I was born. I don't know."

"Mantis, this isn't about you," said Viper. "Po is the one freaking out."

"I'm not freaking out!" replied Po. "I'm freaking in."

But Tigress stopped him before he could protest any further.

"We're here," she said.

The Five turned round. In front of them lay Gongmen City.

THE RETURN OF THE BLACK AND WHITE WARRIOR

Sunrise in Gongmen City saw Shen's wolves ransacking houses for more metal and New Year's fireworks.

Back at the palace, Shen instructed the gorillas to replace his parents' throne with a cannon. Although confident he would be triumphant, Shen still wanted Soothsayer to confirm it.

"Why don't you tell me my fortune now, you silly old goat?" he demanded.

"Come closer, and I will show you. Closer . . . Closer . . ." beckoned Soothsayer. Then, the wise goat began nibbling on Shen's robes!

"That is the finest silk in the province, not a snack!" yelled Shen.

However, Soothsayer used a silk thread stuck in her teeth to create a mysterious smoky vision. "A peacock . . . being stopped by a warrior of black and white," Soothsayer predicted.

The smoke changed, and a Yin Yang consumed the image of the peacock.

"It's impossible and you know it," stated Shen.

"It is not impossible and he knows it," replied Soothsayer, calmly.

"Who?" enquired Shen. Soothsayer pointed to an empty stairway. A second later, Boss Wolf burst in. "Lord Shen! I saw a panda! It fought like a demon. Black and white, big and furry, soft and squishy. Kind of plush and cuddly."

"Find this panda and bring him to me!" screeched Shen.

"So? One panda lives. That does not make you right," argued Shen.

"You're right. Being right makes me right," retorted Soothsayer confidently.

"Then I will kill him, and prove you wrong," said Shen, unaware that Soothsayer had begun chewing his robe again. "Will you stop that!"

Sneaking across the rooftops of Gongmen City, Po and the Five tried to stay out of sight. "We're going to have to do this quietly," Tigress whispered. "That means no marching, no proclaiming and no kung fu." Before Po could open his mouth, she added, "Belly bumps and butt smashes count as kung fu."

"Got it," agreed Po. "Stealth mode," he whispered.

Up on the rooftops, the Five suddenly noticed Po was missing. Tigress spotted a dragon costume bump straight into a fireworks stand, and realized exactly where Po had gone to.

Inside the disguise, Po noticed it was suddenly very hot and cramped. He turned to see the rest of the Five now squashed into the dragon costume with him.

"So," said Crane, "that was stealth mode."

"To be honest," admitted Po, "it's not one of my strongest modes."
From inside the dragon, they watched Shen's wolves terrorize the citizens.

"If we don't get those decorations you're not going to live to see New Year," one wolf soldier growled at a bunny.

"This rice is raw," howled another at a frightened sheep. "Either you cook my rice or I cook you." He didn't care that the sheep couldn't cook anything because they'd stolen everyone's pots and pans.

It was time for payback . . . . The dragon crept up stealthily behind the wolf.

"Hey," said Po, promptly punching the wolf in the face. Pulling the bully inside the mouth of the dragon, the Five dished out kung fu punishment as they passed the wolf down the line, finally 'pooping' him out of the dragon's bottom!

"Who are you?" bleated the surprised sheep.

"We are here to liberate the city and bring Shen to justice," replied Po.

"You will need help," replied the sheep.

In the blink of an eye the dragon 'swallowed' the brave sheep. Inside, he explained that Masters Croc and Ox were being held in Gongmen Jail.

OW THE MI-HTY HAVE FALLEN

Outside the Jail, Mantis made fast work of taking out the prison guards. Once inside, Po peered over the prison balcony and gasped loudly.

"What is it?" Tigress asked.

"Only Master Rhino's greatest student – the brave Master Storming Ox!" replied Po. "Famous for his bravery in the sinking rice fields of the Wing Cho province, when he took on 72 bandits with naught but his bare horns, thereby securing a spot in my book of all-time favourite kung fu heroes."

With one mighty kung fu kick, Tigress took out the door to the cell.

"Come on you guys! Yeah! We're coming for you Shen!" cried Po.

But rather than racing out of the jail to defeat the proud peacock, Master Ox and Master Croc stayed exactly where they were.

"It's too late for that," Master Ox said sadly, as he tried to pull the door of their cell shut.

Po was shocked. "No it's not!" he cried. "Not if we all work together!"

But Masters Ox and Croc would not be persuaded.

"If Master Thundering Rhino could see you now," Po said in dismay.

"You don't know what you're up against," Master Ox said dejectedly. "A lifetime of training gone in an instant," he said, recalling the moment when his fellow Master had been destroyed by one shot from Shen's cannon. "Unless you want the city to suffer, the only honourable thing to do is surrender,' finished Ox.

"Or leave," added Croc.

Po was shocked. Shaking his fists at his former heroes in frustration, he exclaimed, "You stay in your prison of fear, with bars made of hopelessness. And all you get are three square meals a day of shame!"

Boss Wolf and his wolf soldiers flooded the room. "Found you panda!" gloated Boss Wolf, but the Five swiftly took out his wolf soldiers, leaving him feeling a lot less bold.

"Uh oh," he quivered.

"You're mine!!" said Po with relish.

As Boss Wolf turned and fled in fear, Po and the Five followed in hot pursuit.

GOING TO GONGMEN

Po and the Five have set off across China to find Gongmen City. Help them find their way across the grid by using the key below.

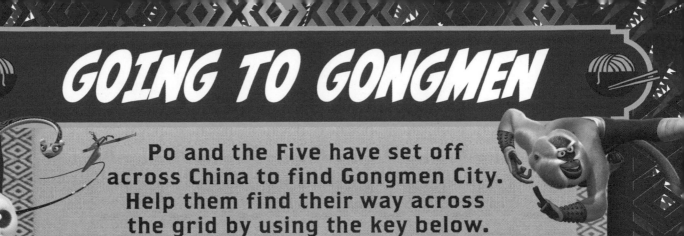

UP **DOWN** **LEFT** **RIGHT**

START

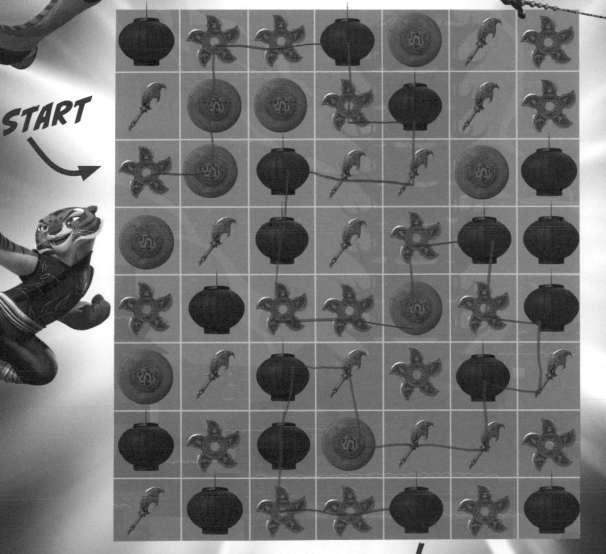

FINISH

ANSWERS ON PAGE 61!

27

PO HAS A PLAN

Outside the jail, Boss Wolf jumped into a nearby rickshaw.

"Get me to the Palace!" he yelled at the scared driver.

But the Five weren't going to let him get away that easily, and were in hot rickshaw pursuit . . .

The driver of Boss Wolf's rickshaw put his foot down and spun sharply round a tight corner. Po was in danger of sailing straight past, but at the last second, Viper snagged Po with her tail and slung him round the bend!

Boss Wolf was so furious he flung the rickshaw driver out and took control himself. He dragged some pedestrians into Po's path, but luckily, the Five snatched them to safety. Suddenly, the wolf threw a basket of baby bunnies at him!

"Yeeeeeee!" yelled Po as the bunnies clung to his face.

No sooner had Po managed to clear the rabbits away from his eyes than the scaffold supporting his rickshaw came to an abrupt end. Po's rickshaw flew through the air and landed on two lantern ropes strung across the street. Po skillfully performed a perfect loop-the-loop before he caught the bunny babies and returned them safely to the carriage.

"Weeeeee! Again! Again!" the baby bunnies cried. Out of the corner of his eye, Po saw the Five race after Boss Wolf's rickshaw. He knew the only way to catch up was to get these bunnies safely out of his carriage.

"Ahh!" Po shouted as an idea came to him "Crane! Catch!"

For the second time that day the clutch of baby bunnies flew straight through the air, but this time, Crane caught them.

"Guys! Give me a shove!" he called to his friends.

Mantis flung Tigress into the air. Mid-flight, Tigress gathered her Chi and in one mighty explosion of energy she connected with Po and sent him hurtling forward at an immense speed.

"Wwawawawawawawawawawal!" cried Po as he landed with an "ooph" in Boss Wolf's rickshaw.

The Dragon Warrior kicked Boss Wolf upright so that his head hit every street sign they passed. But the wolf rebalanced the rickshaw, and then Po's head smacked into the remaining signs!

Finally, the rickshaw hit a ramp and sent the pair flying until they landed with a thud in front of the Palace. Po stood proudly over his defeated foe as the Five joined him.

"Yes! Taste the defeat!" the panda whooped. "Let me tell you something, next time you mess with a panda you better bring a whole ahhhhhh–" Po stopped mid-sentence . . . they were surrounded by Shen's gorillas.

"What are you gonna do now?" sneered Boss Wolf after punching Po in the tummy.

"We surrender!" he answered.

"Po! What are you doing?" Tigress hissed.

"Trust me," Po replied. "I've got a–"

But before he could finish, a gorilla guard had snapped a pair of cuffs around his wrists.

"No way!" cried Po, forgetting about

his plan for a moment. "Eight point acupressure cuffs! Just like the ones that held Tai Lung, the more you move, the tighter they get!"

Po was seriously impressed but the Five were seriously worried as the guards dragged them away to meet Shen.

SO MANY RADISHES!

Mr Ping needs your help to count how many radishes are in the box. You'll need to look very carefully!

ANSWER: 25

ANSWERS ON PAGE 61!

SAY WHAT?

Help Soothsayer complete her prophesy by crossing out all the letters that appear twice or more in the list below.

Shen will be stopped by a warrior of black and White

31

THE FIVE SURRENDER

Inside the Palace, Shen practised his meeting with Po.

"Greetings panda. We meet at last," he said to the mirror. Not satisfied, he tried again. "Greetings panda. At last we meet. No, no, no. Greetings panda, we at last meet . . ." As he unsheathed his blades threateningly, he noticed Soothsayer behind him whilst a gorilla guard looked on.

"You are afraid for a reason," said Soothsayer.

Embarrassed, Shen answered, "I am not afraid. I am just being a gracious host."

From the balcony, Shen and Soothsayer watched the prisoners being led to the tower.

"He's bigger than I expected," said Shen.

"Still, he arrives in chains, so all is well."

"Yes, all is well," replied Soothsayer."

"What do you mean, all is well?" asked Shen.

"I'm simply agreeing with you."

"But did you mean all is well from my point of view or all is well from your point of view?" pushed Shen.

"From the point of the universe," was Soothsayer's answer.

As Po and the Furious Five were led inside the Palace, Po suddenly came face-to-face with an old enemy before him . . . a huge zigzagging stairway! Po had never been, and never would be a fan of stairs.

THE PEACOCK AWAITS

Shen became nervous as huge footsteps and heavy breathing echoed up the stairs. A massive shadow loomed. But instead of a colossal creature, it turned out to be Po being carried by a gorilla.

"Ow!" yelped Po as he was dumped on the floor. "I threw up a little bit on the third landing. Maybe on the twelfth too."

"Greetings panda, at last we mee—" started Shen.

"Hey, how you doing?" Po asked cheerily, deflating Shen's rehearsed menace.

Soothsayer approached Po, and prodded him with her stick. "You've grown up bigger than I thought. Strong. Healthy."

"Look, I don't know who you are but please stand aside sir," said Po.

Viper corrected his friend, "That's a lady."

"Oh. Sorry. The beard threw me. It's kind of misleading," squirmed Po.

"Enough of this nonsense!" bellowed Shen.

As the guards prodded Po and the Five closer, Po leapt at what he thought was Shen's secret weapon. With a chant of "Spear kick!" he shattered what was actually just a tiny model of the cannon.

As Po celebrated, the real cannon, a huge beast of metal towering over him, came into view.

"A lifetime to plot his revenge and he comes to me on his knees," mocked Shen.

But Po was confused. "What? A lifetime? We only heard about Master Rhino a few days ago and we came to avenge him!"

As Viper stealthily picked the locks on Tigress's cuffs, Soothsayer annoyed Po further. "You don't know?" she asked.

"Know what?" answered Po. "OK. You guys are confusing. First the weapon is tiny! Then it's big! Then the goat is a lady, but has a beard! I say we drop all the pleasantries and settle this!"

Shen gave the order to fire the cannon at Po and the Five, but each time his henchmen lit the fuse, Mantis speedily put it out! This gave the Five just enough time to free themselves. Tigress kicked the cannon into the air. It landed barrel-down and blasted a hole through the floor.

Furious, Shen unfurled his tail to reveal his hidden blades, but Po froze at the sight. He saw flashes of memories: a red eye, his mother holding a radish, and . . . Shen surrounded by flames!

"You! You were there," gasped Po.

"Yes. And so were you," sneered Shen

Horrified, Soothsayer and the Five watched as Po let Shen flee through the balcony window.

THE INVASION BEGINS

"You just let Shen get away!" shouted Tigress.

"At least we destroyed the cannon," offered Mantis.

Meanwhile, Shen soared through the night sky to the fireworks factory. Rows of cannons pointed at the Palace Tower.

"Fire!" shouted the peacock.

"Oh, no! He's got more," said Mantis, as cannonballs hurtled towards them – KABOOM! They struck the Palace while Po and the Five ducked and dodged flying chunks of debris.

Another cannon fired at the Palace tower and a lower balcony collapsed, blocking the exit and trapping them all inside.

As the tower began to crumble, Tigress grabbed Po and rushed up the stairs. The team leapt out onto a lower roof of the tower while wolf archers shot flaming arrows at them.

"The only way out is up!" said Tigress, as she blocked the arrows. They reached the top, and jumped over the wolf soldiers just as the tower crashed to the ground.

Inside the fireworks factory, Shen was a very angry peacock indeed.

"You idiot!" he shouted as he smacked his gorilla guard on the nose. "Call in the wolves. All of them. I want them ready to move. The year of the peacock begins now."

"Actually, sir," said Boss Wolf, "this is really the year of the rabbit. There is no peacock."

Shen glared furiously at the wolf and menacingly put one of his blades to the wolf's throat.

"And this is the year, of course, of the peacock. Happy New Year sir," said Boss Wolf sheepishly.

"Get the wolves ready," demanded Shen. "We're loading the ships now!"

Boss Wolf scampered away, barking orders to his army. The preparations for Shen's invasion had begun . . .

FRIENDS OR FOE

As waves of wolves scurried towards the fireworks factory, Po and the Furious Five hid in the shadows outside the jail. Beckoned by howls from the factory, the jail guards raced to join their pack, allowing Po and the Five to sneak inside.

Tigress immediately questioned Po about why he let Shen escape.

"What'd . . . I don't know what you're talking about. I, yeah, okay, he caught me off guard," replied Po, awkwardly.

"The truth," said Tigress. But Po refused to answer her. "Fine. Masters Ox and Croc will keep you far from danger."

"Real far," said Master Croc.

"What?" asked Po, confused.

"You're staying here!" Tigress told him, and the Five turned around to leave.

"Wh . . . Wait! I have to go ba —" Po began to plead.

Tigress whirled around to face him and a hush went over the room. "You're staying here!"

"I'm going and you can't stop me!" Po shouted, as he tried to walk past Tigress.

She grabbed him, twisted him around and threw him back. Po tried again to get past her, but she kicked him into the air and threw him against the wall.

"I have to get to him," said Po.

"Then tell me why!" demanded Tigress.

"He was there, OK?!" replied Po. "The peacock was there the last time I saw my parents. He knows where I came from, who I am. Look, I'm going. I have to understand. The hard-core can't understand."

Tigress's eyes narrowed fiercely and she leapt at Po.

"Tigress! No!" shouted Viper.

But Tigress hugged Po. "The hard-core do understand," she said. "But I can't watch my friend be killed." She turned to the others. "We're going."

The Five walked away, leaving Po with the Masters.

IN THE JAILHOUSE

Tigress needs to get out of jail with the Furious Five – and quickly! Can you guide them through this tricky maze?

START

FINISH

TIGRESS IN TRAINING

Can you draw Tigress in action?
We've started you off . . .

SOOTHSAYER SAYS GOODBYE

Shen watched his wolves prepare for the invasion as Soothsayer was delivered from the Palace by a gorilla guard.

"What shall we do with her?" asked the guard.

"It doesn't matter," Shen replied. "Soon, my ships will sail from Gongmen. Once we reach the ocean, all of China will fall before me."

The peacock pulled an eye-shaped iron from a cauldron of red-hot coals. He pressed it into Gongmen city on the map of China. It sizzled and caught on fire as China burned.

"Then will you finally be satisfied?" asked Soothsayer. "Will the subjugation of the whole world finally make you feel better?"

"It's a start," answered Shen.

"The cup you choose to fill has no bottom. Stop this now, Shen."

"Why on earth would I do that?"

"So your parents can rest in peace."

"My parents hated me. Do you understand?" Shen asked Soothsayer. "They wronged me. I will make it right."

"Goodbye Shen," replied Soothsayer. "I wish you happiness."

"Happiness must be taken," said Shen. "And I will take mine."

Meanwhile, the Furious Five snuck past the armed wolf guards outside the fireworks factory, and took position in sight of its entrance. Looking inside, they spied lots and lots of weapons.

"They loved you," said Soothsayer. "They loved you so much that having to send you away killed them."

Thinking about his parents, Shen became silent. But he pushed his vulnerability away with a steely exterior. "The dead exist in the past," said Shen. "And I must attend to the future."

He turned to the guard and told him to release Soothsayer. "She is no use to me."

"If all of those cannons leave the building, China will fall," said Tigress.

"Then we bring down the building!" said Viper.

"Hey guys!" shouted Mantis. "How about this?" Mantis was perched on top of a barrel, rubbing black powder between his legs before it exploded in his face. "Ow! I'm OK."

"Alright," said Tigress. "Let's go."

PO'S PAST

"What night?" asked Shen.

"*That* night," Po replied.

"Ah, that night. Yes, I was there. Yes, I watched as your parents abandoned you. It's a terrible thing. I believe it went something like this!"

Shen pulled a lever and a suspended bucket swung down, taking out Po.

"Yearggghh!" Po shouted, clutching the bucket by his fingernails as he hung over a pot of molten metal . . .

Po had no intention of staying in the jail with Masters Croc and Ox. He snuck to the factory where wolves moved along the scaffolding. Po vaulted up, landed between two wolves and, with a quick scuffle, knocked them unconscious. Moving them like puppets, he used them as camouflage to get into the factory's rear entrance.

Po wandered through a maze of catwalks before spotting a peacock-shaped shadow.

"Prepare the cannon!" ordered Shen.

Po followed the shadow . . .

"Greetings panda," said Shen, as he unfurled his tail feathers. Po immediately saw the red eye of Shen's tail.

"Argh!" gasped Po. "Tell me what happened that night!"

Meanwhile, the Furious Five leapt through the factory's front entrance, pushing a cart filled with barrels of black powder. Monkey smashed a lantern over the cart and it began to smoulder.

"Here's your New Year's gift!" he said.

"Hope you like it – because you can't return it!" added Mantis.

Suddenly, Po shouted from above. Tigress looked up to see him and Shen.

"Return it! Return it!" shouted Monkey, as the Five frantically extinguished the flames. But wolves soon surrounded them.

"Are you willing to die to find the truth?" posed Shen, as Po struggled back onto the catwalk and faced the peacock.

"You bet I am," said Po. "Though I'd prefer not to." He charged, but Shen flashed his feathers and spun away, kicking Po as he flew by. Po tumbled onto a conveyor belt full of scrap metal on its way to the smelting pot.

Just as he was about to tumble into the smelter, Po stabbed a fork into the conveyor belt and clung to it as it moved along. But the heat from the smelter below singed his bottom.

"Waaaaa! Woooo!" he yelped, as he grabbed a metal wok to protect his rear from the searing heat.

Shen turned as Po rode up the other side of the conveyor belt, armed with pan and fork. Quickly,

Po leapt at Shen, who flashed his tail feathers once more and fled.

"No more running, Shen!" Po bellowed.

"So it seems," replied the peacock.

"Answers! Now!"

"You want to know so badly?" taunted Shen. "You think knowing will heal you, huh? Fill some crater in your soul? Well, here's your answer . . . Your parents didn't love you. But let me heal you."

Shen stood perched in front of a huge cannon. He yanked off the cover and lit the fuse. KABOOM! The Five watched in horror as Po was blown out of the building with nothing but a wok for protection.

PO FINDS THE TRUTH

Po splashed into the river below.

As his unconscious body hit an old dock downriver, somebody prodded him with a stick. Later that night, Po woke up and found himself in an old, rundown hut. In front of a boiling pot, stood . . . Soothsayer!

Po tried to drag himself away, but Soothsayer appeared before him and offered him a cup of tea.

"Yeah, like you could make me drink tha–"

Before Po could finish his sentence,

46

Soothsayer stuck an acupuncture needle in Po's forehead and his jaw dropped open. Soothsayer dumped the contents of the cup into his mouth and removed the needle. Po shut his mouth and swallowed.

"Bleaugh!" squealed Po.

"If I wanted you dead," said Soothsayer, "I would have left you in that river."

"Why save me?" asked Po.

"So you can fulfill your destiny," replied Soothsayer.

"What are you talking about? Where am I? What is this place?"

"I'm surprised you remember so little. But you were so little when it happened . . ."

MAGICAL MEMORIES

Po is trying hard to remember his childhood. How good is your memory? Take a look at all the objects below. Once you think you can remember them all, turn over the page and make a list of all the objects.

CANNON BALL   AXE   SHIELD

LANTERN   BELL   RADISH

PO REMEMBERS

Po looked down at the river running next to the hut. He stared at his reflection in the water. Slowly, Po's memory returned. He saw a panda village where adult pandas harvested radishes and young pandas laughed and played. Baby Po crawled out of the hut to his parents, holding a panda doll.

The village thrived as Young Shen stood in line to rule Gongmen City. Then Soothsayer foretold that someone would stand in his way. A panda. But she never could have foretold what came next . . .

Shen and his wolves ransacked and burned the panda village! Frightened, baby Po sat alone, clutching his doll. Po's dad swung a rake at the invading wolves, hitting Boss Wolf in the eye. They tumbled into Shen, who fell into the fire and singed his claws.

"Take our son! And run away!" Po's dad shouted to Po's mum. She picked up baby Po and ran, whilst the village burned.

Po concentrated . . . he remembered his mum running through a dark forest, pursued by the wolves, their sharp jaws snapping as they ran. As Po's memories gradually returned, he practised Shifu's fluid tai chi movements on a drop of water – working it skillfully from hand to hand.

List all the objects you can remember from page 47

1 _____

2 _____

3 _____

4 _____

5 _____

6 _____

48

Deep in concentration, he saw his mum reach the edge of the forest where she found a radish cart. She hid baby Po amongst the radish baskets, tears streaming down her face as her baby's tiny hands reached out to her. She kissed him and then left him – drawing the wolves and Shen away from the cart.

Po sat alone crying in the rain.

"Your story may not have such a happy beginning, but that doesn't make you who you are," said Soothsayer as she approached Po. "It is the rest of your story. Who you chose to be."

Po thought of his dad, Mr Ping; his quest to become the Dragon Warrior; his friendship with the Furious Five . . .

"So, who are you, panda?" asked Soothsayer.

"I am Po. And I'm gonna need a hat."

THE INVASION

The Furious Five were held captive in chains, aboard Shen's boat.

"Such sad, sad faces," said Shen. "But now is a time only for joy. You are going to be part of something beautiful. Once we reach the harbour, in front of all the world, you and your precious kung fu will die. Then China will know to bow before me."

Shen's boat was part of an enormous armada that floated down the canals of Gongmen city. Shen yanked on a rope and the Five were suspended in mid-air.

"Honestly," sighed Mantis, "even though I'm a kung fu warrior, I always figured my death would be a result of . . . I've told you guys about my dad, right?"

"Yes," replied Viper and Crane.

"We cannot give up hope," said Monkey. "Po would want us to remain strong. Hard-core. Right, Tigress?"

Tigress was silent. A tear rolled down her cheek as she thought of Po.

The boats approached a bridge blocking their way, but Shen used a cannon to blow it to pieces.

"You coward!" Tigress shouted to Shen.

Then she spotted something in the distance – it was Po! Standing on a rooftop, he looked every bit the Dragon Warrior.

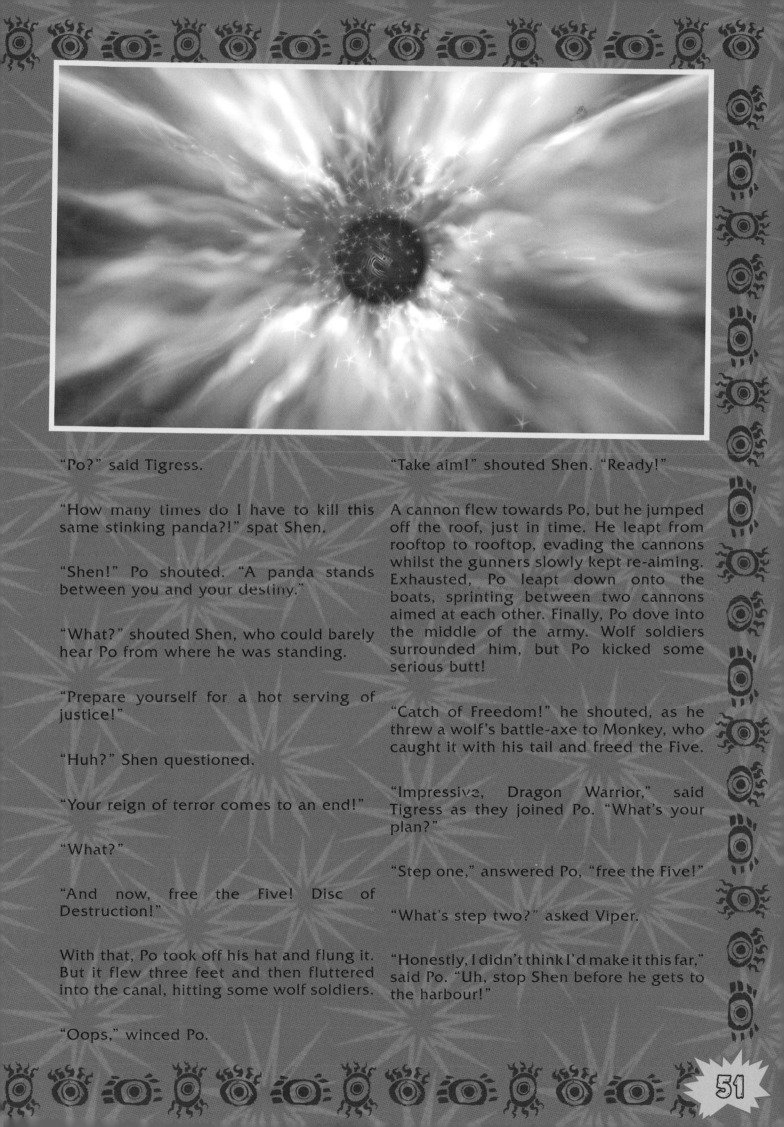

"Po?" said Tigress.

"How many times do I have to kill this same stinking panda?!" spat Shen.

"Shen!" Po shouted. "A panda stands between you and your destiny."

"What?" shouted Shen, who could barely hear Po from where he was standing.

"Prepare yourself for a hot serving of justice!"

"Huh?" Shen questioned.

"Your reign of terror comes to an end!"

"What?"

"And now, free the Five! Disc of Destruction!"

With that, Po took off his hat and flung it. But it flew three feet and then fluttered into the canal, hitting some wolf soldiers.

"Oops," winced Po.

"Take aim!" shouted Shen. "Ready!"

A cannon flew towards Po, but he jumped off the roof, just in time. He leapt from rooftop to rooftop, evading the cannons whilst the gunners slowly kept re-aiming. Exhausted, Po leapt down onto the boats, sprinting between two cannons aimed at each other. Finally, Po dove into the middle of the army. Wolf soldiers surrounded him, but Po kicked some serious butt!

"Catch of Freedom!" he shouted, as he threw a wolf's battle-axe to Monkey, who caught it with his tail and freed the Five.

"Impressive, Dragon Warrior," said Tigress as they joined Po. "What's your plan?"

"Step one," answered Po, "free the Five!"

"What's step two?" asked Viper.

"Honestly, I didn't think I'd make it this far," said Po. "Uh, stop Shen before he gets to the harbour!"

THE FINAL BATTLE

Po and the Five charged into battle, attacking the wolf soldiers around them with their awesome kung fu moves! Suddenly, Masters Ox mad Croc appeared, throwing wolves aside in their wake.

"Master Ox! And Msater Croc! Why did –" started Po.

"Your friend there is very persuasive," answered Master Ox, as Master Shifu flew through the air, his battle staff twirling.

"Master Shifu!" shouted Po.

"Quickly!" said Shifu. "Use their boats to block the way!"

Tigress kicked a cannon, tipping over a boat whilst Po rode on two boats at once, holding them together by their sales.

"I got your back, Po!" shouted Crane as he swept in, flapping his wings and filling the sails. Po steered his two boats into the growing pile of wrecked ships.

"Woohooooyaa!" shouted Po. "Sail of Justice!"

As Po, the Five, Shifu and the Masters leapt into the wolf army, Po smiled.

"I love you guys," he shouted as and the band of heroes fought their way closer and closer to an enraged Shen.

"Why aren't we firing?" Shen asked.

"They're taking out our gunners, sir!" answered Boss Wolf. "They're getting close."

"Fire at them!" ordered Shen, panicked.

"But sir, we'll kill our own!" said the wolf.

"I said fire at them! Fire!"

Blades shot out of Shen's sleeves and he knocked Boss Wolf into the water. Shen leapt onto the cannon himself, aiming it at Po, the Five, Shifu, the Masters, the wolves . . . everyone!

INNER PEACE

The cannon blasted everyone into the air, splashing them into the harbour. Unconscious, Tigress floated past Po, who pulled her to him. Po reached an overturned boat jutting out of the water and climbed onto it, standing in front of the armada.

Shen turned to the gunners. "Let's finish this," he ordered.

Shifu and the Five struggled to get up, helpless as Shen's gunners trained a cannon on Po.

Po slid his feet – the first motion of Shifu's tai chi technique. Po's arms moved fluidly as . . .

"Fire!" shouted Shen.

cool kung fu pose. He looked at his hand – it was on fire!

"Yeeoww!!!" Po yelped, as he shook out the flames.

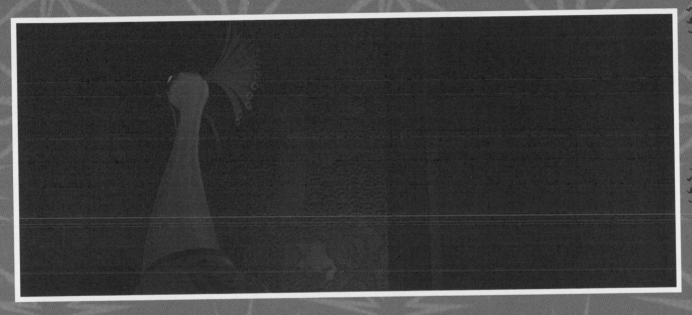

BOOM!

A cannonball sizzled through the air. Po shut his eyes and the cannanball became a drop of water.

"Inner peace . . ." echoed in Po's head. He saw the drop of water bounce, unbroken, off the leaf of a plant. Opening his eyes, he faced the hurtling cannonball.

Po reached out, absorbing the cannonball's momentum, and released it in an altered trajectory. It exploded in the mountains behind him.

As Shen and the wolf army gaped, Tigress smiled in wonder. Po stood in a super-

"Again!" shouted Shen, and more cannons fired. But Po just kept deflecting them away.

"Kill him! Somebody kill him!" yelled Shen.

Boom! Boom! Boom! Cannonballs filled the sky, but they were deflected . . . back at Shen's ships.

"Wait! No!" shouted the peacock. "Cease fire! Cease fire!"

But it was too late . . . A massive cannonball that hurtled at Po, was redirected right back at Shen.

MANO A MANO

As the smoke cleared, Shen looked around at the devastation – his destroyed boats and cannons littered the water.

"How did you...How did you do it?" he asked.

Po shrugged. "You know, you just keep your elbows up, and keep the shoulders loose–"

"Not the cannons," said Shen. "How did you get over it? You lost your parents, everything. It must have scarred you for life."

"See, that's the thing, Shen. Scars heal."

"No, they don't," Shen retorted. "Wounds heal."

"Oh yeah. What do scars do? They fade I guess?"

"I don't care what scars do!"

"You should, Shen," said Po. "You gotta let go of that stuff from the past, because it just doesn't matter. The only thing that matters . . . is what you choose to be now."

"You're right," said Shen, as blades popped out of his robes. "I choose this!"

Shen swung at Po, who dodged his lethal blades. Lightning-fast, Po knocked Shen back, shattering his blades.

"Battle's over," Po told Shen. "You don't have to keep acting all evil!"

Shen's tail unfurled, revealing more blades. He attacked Po, his lethal tail swinging. He threw blades at the panda, but Po blocked them with a wooden plank.

As Shen made a final leap at Po, his tail accidentally sliced the cannon support. Po rolled out of the way just as the cannon landed on top of barrels of explosive black powder . . . KABOOM! Shen was gone.

Po was thrown over the side into the water. As his furry head broke the surface, Tigress reached out and helped him to shore.

From the wreckage of Shen's burning, sinking boat, fireworks shot up into the sky, bathing the citizens of Gongmen in brilliant colours.

As the rest of the Five smothered Po with congratulatory cheers, Po pulled Tigress firmly into the big group hug.

"It seems you have found inner peace. And at such a young age," said Master Shifu, proudly.

"Well, I had a pretty good teacher," smiled Po.

Watching from afar, Soothsayer looked up at the beautiful sky, as the fireworks formed a Yin Yang overhead. "And joy returned to Gongmen."

PO RETURNS TO BALANCE

At Dragon Warrior Noodles and Tofu, Mr Ping tried to deal with an upset pig mother and her son.

"What do you mean he's not here?" she said. "It's my son's birthday. All he wanted was to meet the Dragon Warrior."

"How about some tofu birthday cake instead, ah?" said Mr Ping.

"You know, I think we'll just try again another time. When do you think he'll be back?"

Mr Ping's sad face twitched with emotion. "I don't know, OK? I don't know! Maybe never! I mean, I worry, OK? But that's my job! I'm his dad. At least, I was his dad... Why did he have to go and save China?! I know why, but why?"

"Oh honey," said the pig mum to her son, "he's here!"

Mr Ping turned around and saw Po, holding an armful of radish baskets. He rushed over to his son.

"So, how did it go, son?" asked Mr Ping. "Did you find what you were looking for?"

"Yep," replied Po. "I found out where I came from. I know who I am . . . I am your son." Po pulled his dad into a big bear hug. "I love you Dad."

"I love you too, son. You're probably hungry though. Let me make you something to eat."

"What are you talking about?" asked Po. "I'll cook."

"No, I'll cook."

"Dad—"

"It's the least I can do," said Mr Ping. "You saved China."

"No, it's the least I can do. You raised me."

"Po—"

"Dad—"

"Po—"

"OK," said Po, "how about this — we both cook. Together."

Mr Ping considered this . . .

DO YOU KUNG FU?

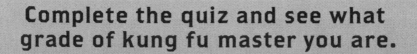

Complete the quiz and see what grade of kung fu master you are.

1. What is Po, the Dragon Warrior's, full name?
   a. Xiao Po
   b. Kung Po
   c. Heng Po

2. What vegetable does Mr Ping *not* use in his soup?
   a. Turnips
   b. Radishes
   c. Bean sprouts

3. How many bean buns can Po fit in his mouth at one time?
   a. 4
   b. 40
   c. 400

4. The Furious Five live in:
   a. The Emerald Castle
   b. The Diamond Fortress
   c. The Jade Palace

5. What sort of animal is the leader of Lord Shen's army?
   a. Rat
   b. Dragon
   c. Wolf

6. The Soothsayer predicted that a warrior of which colours would defeat Shen?
   a. Mauve and black
   b. Pink and green
   c. Black and white

7. Which of these is not a member of the Kung Fu Council of Gongmen City?
   a. Master Weeping Willow
   b. Master Thundering Rhino
   c. Master Storming Ox

8. What sort of weapon does Lord Shen use to try and take control of Gongmen City?
   a. Sword
   b. Cannon
   c. Ninja star

9. What must Po find to help him defeat Lord Shen?
   a. Inner strength
   b. Inner happiness
   c. Inner peace

10. What is one of Po's favourite kung fu moves?
    a. Feet of Fury
    b. Ears of Anger
    c. Tails of Terror

SCORES: 0-3: You have much to learn!   4-7: You have the kung fu skills of a master!   8-10: You and the Dragon Warrior are one!

ANSWERS

Page 10:
B

page 31:
WHITE

Page 11: From top to bottom
D, E, G, B, C, A, F

Page 40:

Page 27:

START
FINISH

START
FINISH

Page 30:
24

Page 60: 1–a, 2–b, 3–b, 4–c, 5–c, 6–c, 7–a, 8–b, 9–c, 10–a